D0246950

Jewish (misc. countries)

withdrawn

The Prince
Who Thought
he was a Rooster

and other
Jewish Stories

For Natasha, Katie, Louise, Catherine, Lyndsey and Andrew

The Prince Who Thought he was a Rooster and other Jewish Stories
Copyright © Frances Lincoln Limited 2007
Text copyright © Ann Jungman 2007
Illustrations copyright © Sarah Adams

First published in Great Britain and the USA in 2007 by
Frances Lincoln Children's Books, 4 Torriano Mews,
Torriano Avenue, London NW5 2RZ
www.franceslincoln.com

British Library Cataloguing in Publication Data available on request

ISBN: 978-1-84507-793-8

Printed in Singapore

1 3 5 7 9 8 6 4 2

The Prince
Who Thought
he was a Rooster

and other Jewish Stories

Retold by Ann Jungman
Illustrated by Sarah Adams

Introduction by Michael Rosen

FRANCES LINCOLN
CHILDREN'S BOOKS

Contents

Introduction   6

The Chilli Champion   9
Morocco

No Room to Swing a Cat   16
Russia

The Golem of Prague   23
Former Czechoslovakia

Friends for Life   34
Tunisia

How Does it Feel?   42
Poland

King for Three Days   49
Germany

The Coat of Memories   56
Russia

The Prince Who Thought he was a Rooster   62
Poland

The Hundred Faces of the Tsar   71
Russia

The Silent Princess   78
Morocco

Sources   86

Introduction

For several thousand years there have been people who've described themselves as Jews. There's hardly a country in the world where some Jews haven't settled for a while or even for centuries. Wherever this has happened, the Jews living, working and worshipping there have influenced the country they've been in whilst absorbing ideas and culture from those around them.

In other words, 'Jews' covers a wide variety of peoples, and as with all religions, there are many different ways for Jews to worship, observe their festivals, or indeed to live a life acknowledging that they've inherited something from their Jewish background.

Jews have always had much in common with the Christians and Muslims amongst whom they've lived but religious tensions have often boiled over, leaving them isolated and sometimes persecuted.

All oppressed people feed their experiences into their stories, and the Jews are no exception. So, in the sixteenth-century story *The Golem of Prague*, the powerless Jews create a monster to reclaim power – power which, in reality, they didn't have. At other times they have told funny stories such as *The Prince Who Thought he was a Rooster* and *The Chilli*

Champion, for laughter blocks out fear and resentment.

In some of their stories, they have absorbed tales told by their non-Jewish neighbours and introduced into them a clever Jewish character who becomes the King's chief advisor and governs wisely and well – *The Hundred Faces of the Tsar* is an example of this. And, of course, some Jewish stories are about feelings, such as sadness in *The Coat of Memories* and despair in *How Does it Feel?*

Jewish communities (including my own, the Ashkenazim of Poland and Russia) have always coped with unhappiness by developing jokes and comic tales. Some of these are self-mocking, laughing at the anxieties of their insecure lives and at their loving but strict mothers who keep the home together.

Telling stories is one way we have of sharing things we care about. This book makes visible some delicious stories which would otherwise float away in the steam coming off chicken soup. So, enjoy!

Michael Rosen

The Chilli Champion

"I'm bored," announced the King. "I am very, very bored."

"Oh dear," said the Grand Vizier. "That will never do, Your Majesty. What can we organise, O Great One, to divert you? A wrestling competition, perhaps?"

"I'm sick of wrestling," grumbled the King.

"A horse race?" suggested the Queen.

"Boring," replied her husband.

"I know – a tournament," piped up the Prince. "I love tournaments."

"Well, I don't," declared the King. "I want a competition that is new and different, something that has never happened before."

Suddenly a smile lit up his face.

"I've got it. Yes! Oh, it will be such a laugh.

I really am a very clever king. Grand Vizier, go to the Christians and tell them to send a champion to the palace. Then go to the Muslims and tell them the same thing — and yes, why not go and tell the Jews too! I want them all to present their champions here this afternoon, without fail. If they don't, the consequences for them will be grim."

"What kind of a champions do you require, O Light of the World?" asked the Grand Vizier nervously. "A fighter? A horseman? A runner?"

"Oh… just a champion," said the King vaguely, and, singing happily to himself, he wandered off.

The Grand Vizier rushed off to find the Imam.

"The King commands you to send a champion representing Muslims to the palace this afternoon. If you do not fulfil his command, terrible things will happen to you all."

"No problem," came the reply. "We'll send Yussef. He's as big as a tree and as strong as an ox. Tell His Majesty that we will be there."

Next the Grand Vizier went to the Archbishop, saying, "The King commands you to send a champion to represent Christians at the palace this afternoon. Should you fail to do so, every Christian in this land will regret it."

"We have a worthy champion in Sir Grizzlebert," said the Archbishop." No man can wield a sword or ride a horse like him. Tell the King to expect him this afternoon."

The Grand Vizier was just making his way back to the palace, when he remembered he still had to ask the Jews for a champion.

"I don't know why the King wants them there," thought the Vizier. "It's very odd, but orders are orders."

And he went off to the Jewish quarter of the city.

"Take me to the Rabbi," he demanded.

When the Rabbi heard the royal command, he summoned all the Jews together.

"We have to send a champion to the King this afternoon. Whom do you suggest?"

"But, Rabbi, we don't have any champions," they said. "We aren't like that — we don't have big, strong fighters."

"Well, you must send someone," the Grand Vizier told them. "Our King, May His Name Be Praised, insists on it. If you fail, the consequences for you will be grim."

Suddenly a shrill voice piped up from the back of the crowd, "Let me be our champion!"

"Don't be ridiculous, Isaac," snapped the Rabbi. "You are old and decrepit. What use would you be?"

"None," agreed the old man, "but someone has to go, and I am a widower with no children and near the end of my life. What have I to lose but my life? Come on — you know it makes sense."

And so it was, that later that day Yussuf, Sir Grizzlebert and Isaac made their way into the King's court, where all the courtiers and supporters had assembled.

When the crowd saw Isaac, they roared with laughter.

"A champion? That little weed?" they shouted. "You must be joking."

The King stood and held up his hand for silence.

"This is a competition with a difference,"

he announced. "The champion will be the one who can eat a hot chilli without yelling *"Ooooo-oooow!"* or begging for water. Now, offer them the chilli peppers!"

And the trumpets played as a page carried out a silver platter with three red chilli peppers arranged on it.

Yussef took one, crunched it – and then ran around yelling, *"Ooooo-oooow!* Water, give me water! I'm burning up! Water…"

"Take him away," commanded the King.

Sir Grizzlebert smiled in a superior way. "Give me a pepper, boy. I'm tough. I can handle it."

But he took a bite, went red, held his throat, staggered back and then shouted, *"Oooooh-oooow!* Help! Water – give me water, for mercy's sake!"

"Take him away!" yelled the King. "Ha, only the old Jew left. This should be fun."

Isaac took the chilli, bit into it, and started to sing:

"It's because I am a Jew-oooooo
That I have to chew-ooooo!
I'll need to go to the loo-oooo
Before I'm through-ooo!
I'm telling you-oooo

*This chilli's red hue-oooo
Nearly blew-oooo
My mind!"*

And he swallowed the last bit of chilli.

"The man is amazing," declared the King. "Where others moaned and begged, he just sang a delightful song. Not a 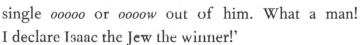 single *ooooo* or *ooooow* out of him. What a man! I declare Isaac the Jew the winner!'

As Isaac left the courtyard, to deafening cheers, he whispered to the Rabbi, "Do you really think the King didn't notice all the *"oooos"* in my song?"

"Who knows?" smiled the Rabbi."But you were brilliant, Isaac. You deserve to be a hero!"

No Room to Swing a Cat

Mordecai was a poor Jewish farmer who lived with his wife Leah in a tiny hut. The two of them managed to scratch a living from the two small fields that surrounded their modest home. There was just enough space and just enough to eat for the two of them. The couple were the most discontented couple in the village, always moaning and complaining about their lot in life. Then Leah's mother got so old, she had to come and live with them.

There was only one room in the miserable hut.

Mordecai sighed.

"Oh dear, nothing for it — I shall have to put a curtain across this tiny room."

Behind the curtain they put Leah's mother's huge bed. The hut, which had always seemed small, now felt hopelessly overcrowded. Mordecai and Leah were even more miserable than usual.

"Your mother snores at night and keeps me awake," moaned Mordecai.

"I know," said Leah. "And she interferes with my cooking, and I can't move in my own kitchen."

"I don't know how long I can go on like this," complained Mordecai.

"I'm at the end of my tether too," agreed Leah. "I think we should go and talk to the Rabbi. He's a clever, educated man. He will know what to do."

Mordecai brightened up at this suggestion, and together they walked over to the Rabbi's house and poured out their woes.

The Rabbi listened intently, thought for a long time and then said, "Do you have any livestock?"

"Well, yes," replied Mordecai. "Quite a lot – chickens and so on."

"Good," nodded the Rabbi. "Now what you need to do is to bring the chickens into your house, and soon all your troubles will be over."

Leah and Mordecai stared at each other in amazement.

"Rabbi, did you say to bring the chickens into the house?" they asked.

"Yes. Do as I say, and all will be well."

So the couple did as the Rabbi said, and soon the house was full of chickens. They were noisy and smelly and laid eggs in inconvenient places and jumped up on the table and ate food not meant for them, when Mordecai and Leah weren't looking.

Then the rooster started to sleep on the bedpost and woke them up with a deafening *Cock-a-doodle-doo!* early each morning.

Mordecai rushed back to the Rabbi.

"Rabbi, Rabbi, Leah and I did exactly what you told us and everything is ten times as bad as before!" he cried.

"Aha," said the Rabbi, nodding. "That is unfortunate. Do you have a cow?"

"We do, sir," Mordecai told him. "But what has that got to do with anything?"

"Take the cow into the house and tie it to the door. Then you will see – all your troubles will soon be over."

Mordecai trudged back home and told Leah what the Rabbi had said.

"It sounds very odd to me," commented Leah,

"but the Rabbi is a wise man, and we must take his advice."

So the cow was brought in and tied to the door. No one could go in or out without pushing the cow out of the way. The cow didn't like being inside and made a lot of noise and ate the best curtains.

"I've had enough!"shouted Leah after a week. "I'm going to see the Rabbi myself."

And she stormed out of the house.

"Rabbi," she cried, "what are you doing to us? Everything is a hundred times worse than it was before. What shall we do?"

"You have a goat?" asked the Rabbi.

"We do," she told him, and her heart sank. "Do you want us to bring the goat into the house too?"

"Yes," nodded the Rabbi. "Tie the goat to the end of the bed and soon all your troubles will be over."

Leah hurried back to their miserable hut, pushed the cow to one side, trod on an egg and slipped, and shouting over the noise of the chickens, told Mordecai, "He says bring the goat in and tie it to the end of the bed."

"Oh dear," said Mordecai, burying his head in his hands. "That sounds completely crazy to me, but the Rabbi is the Rabbi – he is an educated man and we must do what he says."

So the goat was brought in to add to the chaos.

At dawn the next day Mordecai and Leah, who hadn't had a moment's sleep, went to the Rabbi's house.

"Rabbi," they told him, "we cannot live like this. The goat smelled so bad, we didn't get a wink of sleep last night. What can we do to restore the peace of our little home?"

"I'll tell you what to do," announced the Rabbi. "Put all the animals back outside where they belong, scrub your house from top to bottom, and in two days come back and tell me how you feel."

When Mordecai and Leah returned two days later, they were smiling and cheerful.

"How is it?" asked the Rabbi.

"Quiet and peaceful and clean," they told him, beaming happily.

"And Leah's mother, she doesn't take up too much room?"

"Of course not," cried Leah. "Just the two of us

and one old lady — there's plenty of space. It's a little palace."

"Like paradise," agreed Mordecai. "We shall never complain again."

After that, Mordecai and Leah were much happier. They stopped moaning and began to laugh and joke with their neighbours.

"I don't know what the Rabbi said to those two," commented the neighbours, "but whatever it was, it certainly worked!"

The Golem of Prague

Hundreds of years ago, in the beautiful city of Prague, there lived a Rabbi famous for his wisdom and piety, Rabbi Judah Loew. It was not a happy time for the Jews of Prague because a monk called Thaddeus was stirring up bad feeling among the Christians against the Jewish population.

"Why do we need these strangers in our midst," he said to the crowds, "these people who killed Christ? Let's get rid of them. Prague will be a better place without them."

Every night the Jews were shut into a small walled area called the Ghetto, and outside they could hear the shouts of angry crowds who had been listening to Thaddeus calling for their blood. The Jews crowded together, vulnerable and scared, and turned to their Rabbi for advice.

"Rabbi Loew," they cried, "what shall we do

if Thaddeus's mob breaks down the gates and tries to kill us in our beds?"

"Be calm," the Rabbi told them. "The Emperor is on our side and he will make sure that there are enough soldiers to control the crowd."

"Why does Thaddeus hate us so, Rabbi?" asked a girl in tears. "What harm did we ever do to that monk?"

"That is a hard question to answer," sighed Rabbi Loew. "I think Thaddeus sees it as a way to gain power and I think he doubts his own faith. Seeing the Jews, who have a different religion, makes him doubt himself even more. Poor Thaddeus thinks that if he gets rid of us he will get rid of his doubts — but about that, as everything else, he is wrong."

That summer there was a very bad harvest and over the winter food was short.

"Blame the Jews!" thundered Thaddeus to the hungry people. "This is their fault. They poisoned the wells and killed the animals. Death to the Jews!"

"Why do they listen to such nonsense?" the terrified Jews asked Rabbi Loew. "We were all here in Prague when the crops died in the fields. We had nothing to do with it. It was the terrible weather."

"When people are hungry and angry, they need to find someone to blame," the Rabbi told them sadly, "and a minority that is unarmed is the ideal scapegoat."

"Maybe we should be armed," said the Rabbi's son-in-law.

"We wouldn't stand a chance," replied the Rabbi. "We are outnumbered a thousand to one. And remember the great commandment, the greatest of all: *Thou shalt not kill.*"

That night, as the Rabbi slept, he had a dream. In this dream he went down to the river and made a giant out of clay, and he gave the giant life by uttering some sacred words over it.

When he woke up, the Rabbi remembered his dream and wondered if God had been talking to him in his sleep.

Outside the walls of the Ghetto, Thaddeus continued to spread his poison of hate and as Easter approached, the Rabbi grew more worried. After a while he sent his son-in-law out into the crowd in disguise to listen to what the evil monk was saying.

"Citizens of Prague," shouted Thaddeus, "my hungry friends, who is to blame for your sad condition?"

"The Jews!" chorused the crowd.

"You speak truly, my friends," continued the monk, "and now we are in even greater danger from that vile race. For as we near our feast of Easter, their Passover is approaching. Now, at Passover the Jews eat a special flat bread called *matzos*, and this *matzos* is made with nothing less than the blood of innocent Christian children."

The crowd were horrified.

"Do you want to lose your children to the blood lust of the Jews?" demanded Thaddeus.

"No!" yelled the crowd. "Protect our little ones from the perfidious Jews."

Levi, the Rabbi's son-in-law could keep silent no longer.

"Don't listen to him," cried Levi. "He is telling you wicked lies. *Matzos* is made from flour and water and no yeast. It has no blood in it, not one drop. Come and watch us make it if you have doubts."

"He lies, he lies!" thundered Thaddeus. "Beat him for misleading you."

So they set upon Levi, and if the Emperor's men had not come along and intervened, he might have died.

That evening, seeing the bruised and battered Levi, Rabbi Loew remembered his dream about the giant made from clay.

"Maybe the time has come for me to create this giant," he thought sadly. "Although the creation of new life is only meant to be for God, I think in my dream God was telling me that in these desperate circumstances, I could be God just for once."

So Rabbi Loew got out his most sacred books, the Kabbalah, which only the greatest scholars and the wisest of men ever read. He studied for many days, shut away in his room over the synagogue.

On the third night he asked his fellow-scholar Cohen and his son-in-law Levi to come with him secretly to the edge of the Vlatava river. By the light of one small lamp, the three men set about making a giant out of clay.

"We are making a Golem," the Rabbi told them, "a clay giant to protect the Jewish people, and I will give him life with magic words from the Kabbalah."

They worked all night, and at first light a huge, ugly clay figure lay on the river bank.

The Rabbi wrote down the Words of Life in Hebrew on a piece of paper and put it in the Golem's mouth.

The huge figure moved a bit, then yawned and sat up.

"I shall not give this Golem the power of speech. He is not a man, he does not have a soul, he does not have knowledge of God – May His Name Be Praised – and he does not know right from wrong."

So they took the Golem back with them to the Ghetto and the Jews felt more secure with the giant in their midst. The Golem seemed quite happy to do the heavy work that it would take five men to do. Each night the Rabbi took the paper out of the Golem's mouth, and he turned back into a lifeless clay shape again.

Then one night, Thaddeus led a huge crowd to the gates of the Ghetto and they tried to break down the gate. Terror spread through the streets as the bloodthirsty cries of the crowd surrounded the Ghetto.

"We must use our Golem," cried Levi. "This is what we made him for."

"No," insisted Rabbi Loew. "The Golem is made of clay. He has no soul. If we let him loose, goodness knows what horrors he may act out. No. I will send a message to our Emperor to ask for help. The Emperor is no admirer of Thaddeus and his mob."

"If help comes, it may come too late," Levi pointed out. "Our people are terrified."

The Rabbi shook his head. "I cannot take responsibility for what the creature may do."

While the Rabbi went off to pray, Levi took the paper with the Words of Life on it and put it in the Golem's mouth. Then he led the Golem to the gates.

Hearing all the noise and seeing the torches in the night sky, the Golem grew very excited and he rushed out, picked up the nearest person and flung him over the heads of the crowd. The crowd looked at the monster in shock and disbelief. They had never seen anything like it.

Then the Golem grabbed a stick and started laying into the crowd. Thaddeus took one look at the giant and ran away as fast as he could, and the rest of the mob followed.

"The Jews have got a monster to defend them!" they shrieked. "Help, run for it!"

The Jews cheered.

Hearing all the noise, Rabbi Loew ran as fast as he could to the gates. To his horror, he saw the dead and the wounded, and the Golem grinning happily.

The Rabbi rushed over and took the paper from the Golem's mouth, and the grinning creature turned to clay again.

"We must destroy this creature and never make another," said the Rabbi, "for he does our evil deeds for us. Look at the number of dead! I am responsible for this, and I will have to live with the knowledge of it until my dying day."

So they carried the Golem to a room above the synagogue. There the Rabbi dismantled the giant, came out and locked the door behind him. No one has ever been into that room since.

The next day, the Emperor summoned Rabbi Loew, for he had heard the story of the giant who had protected the Jews.

The Rabbi told the Emperor the whole story. "Now I realise I was wrong to take on the role of God and create life. It will never happen again."

"You are a man of great wisdom, Rabbi, and I shall see to it that your people are not threatened in this way again. I have ordered my soldiers to distribute food to the poor. Thaddeus lost all his power last night when he was the first to flee. With God's help, you will never need another Golem."

If you go to Prague today, the synagogue of Rabbi Loew still stands there and is a major tourist attraction, but the door to the room that is supposed to contain the Golem's remains remains firmly locked – and no one has ever made a Golem since that day.

Friends for Life

In Tunis, there lived two boys who were the closest of friends from the moment they could walk. Aaron was a Jew and Memet was a Muslim. Every day they played together, and no one ever saw one of them without the other appearing moments later.

The two boys grew up into fine, strong men. Memet got married and Aaron lived next door and often ate with Memet and his wife. All went well until, one day, war broke out. The country was attacked from the east and from the west.

Both men rushed to join the army. Memet was sent to fight in the East and Aaron was sent to the West. By a strange chance, both men were taken prisoners by different armies in different countries and held as hostages.

Memet was freed first and as soon as he got home,

he said to his wife, "I hear that Aaron is being held by the King of the West. My father does business there, so I'll go and see if I can free him." Memet's wife was sad that her husband had to leave again, but she knew what great friends they were, and she agreed.

When Memet arrived in the Kingdom of the West, he began to do business and soon made a lot of money. But the King of the West had spies everywhere. One of the spies ran to the King.

"Sire, sire, there is a merchant here from the country we've been at war with. Some of his behaviour is very suspicious. We think he may be a spy."

"A spy?" shouted the King, "A spy dares to come to my land disguised as a merchant? Arrest him this minute and bring him to me."

So Memet was dragged before the King,

"You miserable creature," snapped the King. "How dare you come to my land and spy on my people? Why are you asking so many questions about this one and that one?"

"Your Highness, I have a great friend in your country who was taken prisoner in the war. I have come to pay for his release," Memet answered.

The King laughed heartily.

"Do you expect me to believe such nonsense? I think you are a spy and you shall be treated like one. Take him away, and in the morning execute him."

"Sire," cried Memet, "You have a reputation as a fair man. Please hear me out."

"I give you one minute," declared the King.

"I have a wife and children, with another child on the way. Please let me go home and settle my affairs and make sure my family is taken care of. After that, I will return to receive my punishment."

The King laughed again,

"Now I know you are a joker. You don't seriously expect me to believe that you will come back here to be executed, do you?"

"Yes, Your Majesty. And as a form of insurance, my friend will be willing to die in my place if I don't return on the appointed day."

This time the King nearly split his sides, and he laughed until the tears ran down his face.

"A friend who loves you enough to die in your place? Oh dear, this fellow really is such a comedian! And who is this noble-hearted friend of yours?"

"His name is Aaron, and you are holding him as a prisoner-of-war."

The King asked his servants, "Are we holding someone of that name?"

"Yes, Sire," replied the gaoler.

"Then bring the man here," ordered the King.

So Aaron was brought before the King and the two old friends greeted each other warmly

"Aaron," said the King, "your friend here is condemned to death as a spy."

"Oh no!" cried Aaron, going white. "Please spare him, Sire."

"I have agreed to let your friend Memet go home to sort out his affairs and take care of his family," declared the King, "on condition that, should he fail to return, you will die in his place. I cannot believe that any man would agree to such an arrangement. Am I right?"

"No, Sire. My friend is a man of honour and will return – and if he does not, I will die in his place."

The entire court gasped in amazement.

The King looked perplexed, but said to Memet, "Well, Mr Spy, you had better get going – but be back in two weeks, or your friend's head will roll."

"Sire," said Memet, "I assure you I'll be back. Aaron, I'll see you soon! I will make sure you go home a free man."

The friends embraced, and Memet set off.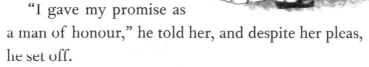

"Arrange an execution in two weeks," ordered the King, "for this poor man Aaron has been abandoned by his so-called friend."

When Memet got home, he made sure his wife and children were well provided for. His wife begged him not to go back, but Memet insisted.

"I gave my promise as a man of honour," he told her, and despite her pleas, he set off.

But a few days later, he fell ill of a fever and became delirious. He slept for days. Eventually he woke up and asked, "What day is it?"

When he realised that the following day was the date fixed by the King for his execution, he jumped on his horse and rode all day and night.

As he galloped into the King's palace, he saw that a big crowd had gathered for the execution. And there was Aaron, with his hair cut short, kneeling to await the executioner's blow.

"Stop! Stop the execution!" shouted Memet. "I am back now. Let my friend go."

Aaron rose to his feet, ran forward and pulled Memet from his horse.

"You idiot, why did you come back? I would have died instead of you. After all, you have a family who need you. Run! please, run for your life!"

"No," replied Memet. "I cannot let you die in my place, Aaron. It would not be honourable, and I gave my word. Now be off – and let the King execute me."

And soon the two friends were rolling in the dust, fighting for the right to be executed.

The King could not believe his eyes. Then he began to laugh.

"Stop the fight," he commanded.

The two men were dragged apart, looking daggers at each other.

"Memet, Aaron, your love and honour have really impressed me. The world is a better place for having men like you in it, men of honour willing to sacrifice themselves. So now you are both free to go. And I shall make peace with your King, for if the men in your country are anything like you two, it is a country to have as an ally, not an enemy. Go in peace."

So the two friends returned home and remained the best of friends for the rest of their lives.

How Does it Feel?

Long ago, in a small town in Poland, a poor Jewish tailor was sitting on the floor of his home, sewing. Suddenly the door was flung open and a small, fat man in army uniform rushed in.

"Quick, quick, hide me, I beg you!" cried the little man. "Half the Russian army is after me. Please – I can pay you – but they will be here any minute."

The little fat man looked so scared that the tailor took pity on him.

"Under the quilt," cried the tailor. "It's a good thick one. Lie on your back and stay as still as you can."

"Thank you, thank you," breathed the soldier. Outside, they could hear the sound of horses' hooves getting closer.

Without even taking off his boots, the man leapt

under the quilt and the tailor covered him up – just as the door was kicked in. Quickly the tailor went back to his sewing, and when eight Russian soldiers tumbled into the room, he looked up in surprise.

"You, Jew, have you seen a fat little Frenchman in an army uniform pass this way?"

"I have seen nothing, gentlemen. I just sit here sewing and, as you can see, I have very little here. What would a French soldier want with me?"

"True enough," agreed the Russian. "But we saw Napolcon running for his life, and he ran towards this town."

"Napoleon?" said the Jew. "No, I've never met him. He can't be a local man."

The soldiers all laughed.

"No, he's not a local, that's for sure. The Emperor Napoleon is the most powerful man in the world. He's the ruler of France and half of Europe."

"Never heard of him," said the Jew. "What do you want him for?"

"You are an ignorant, stupid man," shouted the officer. "Don't you know that Napoleon invaded Russia with the biggest army ever? But we defeated him. His French army couldn't stand the cold and frost. We've got those Frenchies on the run and

we've got the great man on the run too, like a common criminal. Now we want to take him prisoner."

"Search my house," said the tailor. "As you can see, I live a simple life – there aren't many places to hide in here."

The soldiers looked in every nook and cranny and were just leaving, when one soldier ran over to the bed and stuck his bayonet into the quilt three times.

The tailor stared at the floor, feeling a bit sick.

"No emperor here, sir," said the soldier.

"Right, let's go. Napoleon can't be far away. Search every house."

When all the soldiers had gone, the Jew stared at the quilt. Slowly it was pushed aside, and Napoleon emerged.

"Are you all right?" whispered the tailor.

"I'm fine," said Napoleon, pulling his jacket down and putting his hat on. "I presume you were joking when you said you hadn't heard of me."

"Oh no, Your Honour," replied the Jew. "I lead a very quiet life here. I don't know what goes on outside my little town."

"How extraordinary!" mused Napoleon. "Someone who has not heard of me. My good man,

I am the greatest general and the greatest ruler in the world, and you have saved my life. Now, give me three wishes and I will grant them. Anything you like."

The tailor thought for a minute and then said, "Well, sir, if it would not be too much trouble, could I have a new roof?"

"A new roof?" asked the Emperor faintly. "Is that really what you want?"

"Oh yes, sir, yes indeed. It gets very cold here in the winter. A good roof is a wonderful thing for a poor man."

"Here's a purse of gold for your roof. Now, think hard before you ask for your second wish. You can have houses, honours, money, jewels, a high position – what will it be?"

The Jew thought for a minute, and then said,

"I am to be married soon. An outside well would be wonderful for my wife-to-be."

"A well?" shouted Napoleon. "I offer you riches and honours, and all you want is a well? What a lack of imagination! What a lack of ambition! Here's a purse for your well. Now, come on man, make a sensible wish for your last request."

Again the Jew thought for a minute, and then he said, "I would like to know how you felt under that quilt when the Russians were digging around with their bayonets."

Just then, a group of French soldiers rushed in and knelt before Napoleon.

"Oh, Emperor, Emperor , you are safe! Glory be to God!" And one by one they kissed his hand. "You must come with us now, Highness. Your army needs to know that you are still alive."

"One minute," said Napoleon. "There is the small matter of this ridiculous fellow to deal with. I offered him riches, position, jewels – anything he wanted – and he asked me a stupid question. Take him away, put him in a cell, and tomorrow morning at dawn, shoot him."

The soldiers bustled the protesting Jew out of his house, back to the barracks, and locked him up.

All night the tailor tossed and turned. He couldn't sleep. He wouldn't eat. After a while he asked for some paper and wrote letters to his parents and fiancée. Then he prayed.

At dawn they took him outside and stood him against a wall.

The tailor came out in a sweat and his knees felt as if they would give way under him. He closed his eyes and waited for the shot.

But it never came.

Then he felt a hand on his shoulder.

"Come on, Jew, you're still here. It's all right. You're free to go. By the way, the Emperor asked us to give you this."

The tailor opened the envelope and read:

You wanted to know how I felt.
Well, now you do.

Napoleon

King for Three Days

Long ago in the great city of Worms, in Germany, a knight on horseback was shouting at an old man.

"Give me your blessing, old man," yelled Count Godfrey de Bouillon to Rashi, the most famous Rabbi of his day, who was standing in front of him. "Give me your blessing – or you die!"

"You don't frighten me, Sir Godfrey," smiled the Rabbi. "I am old and ready to meet my God."

Sir Godfrey was so surprised, he just stared at the old man. Then he shouted, "We are on our way to the Holy Land, to free the great city of Jerusalem from the Muslims. For this, you Jews should be grateful and bless our mission."

The Rabbi smiled again.

"Sir Godfrey, my people live among the Muslims in Jerusalem. We live in peace and worship freely at our holy places. You, on the other hand, will kill every non-Christian you come across on your way to Jerusalem. You leave a trail of blood, Crusader. There is no way I can bless your enterprise."

The knight could not believe his ears.

"I am Sir Godfrey de Bouillon, the greatest warrior in Europe. I have been chosen to lead this great Crusade. Who do you think you are, to talk to me like that? I insist that you give me your blessing."

Three of Sir Godfrey's largest knights grabbed Rashi and held him in an iron grip.

"Blessings are not in the gift of man: they are bestowed by Heaven on worthy objects," replied the Rabbi. "And why do you need a blessing from a humble Rabbi, when all your priests have given you their approval?"

"You have the reputation of being a truly holy man," said the knight angrily. "If you cannot give me your blessing, then tell me the future. I have tens of thousands of men under my command. Will I succeed in recapturing Jerusalem for the Christian faith?"

"You will succeed – and then you will fail," the Rabbi told him.

"What is that supposed to mean?" demanded the knight with a sneer.

"You will capture Jerusalem and you will become the king of that city."

"So I will succeed! Thank you, old man. You have raised my spirits."

Sir Godfrey turned to go.

"But you will be king for only three days," Rashi called after him.

Sir Godfrey went white and turned back to look at the Rabbi.

"Will I return to this place from the Holy Land?"

"You will." nodded the Rabbi. "Oh yes, you will return – but not at the head of a triumphant army as you dream of. No, you will return with just three men."

Sir Godfrey roared with laughter,

"What, old man, are you trying to scare me? Is this your revenge because I have been killing Jews and other non-believers on my way to Jerusalem? What nonsense! Three men indeed! But beware, Jew, when I do return, if even one small part of your prophecy is wrong, you will die!"

And with that, he jumped on his horse and rode away laughing.

Some months later, Sir Godfrey laid siege to Jerusalem and eventually the city fell to his knights. On taking the city, the Crusaders killed every person in Jerusalem – man, woman and child. At the end of the day the soldiers were knee-deep in the blood of the thousands they had murdered. The Crusaders all gathered in the main square and offered the throne of Jerusalem to Sir Godfrey.

That night Sir Godfrey went to bed happy, but in the morning, when he woke up and saw the bare red hills around Jerusalem and the sun beating down, he suddenly felt homesick.

"If I stay here," he thought, "I shall never see the green fields and the grey skies of my dear France again." So two days later he said to his men, "You have done me a great honour inviting me to be your king, but I feel that I belong in Europe. I shall continue to fight for a while in this land against the Muslim enemy, but afterwards I shall lead a victorious army home."

That night, Sir Godfrey suddenly remembered Rabbi Rashi's prediction.

"I was King just for three days, as the Rabbi said," he thought. "Still, that is merely a coincidence. Rashi's predictions were nonsense. He was just trying to scare me."

Within months Sir Godfrey and his army began their journey home. On the way they were caught up in a number of battles and ambushes, disease broke out, and many men died for lack of water in the heat.

The army that approached Worms was a tiny contingent of thin, tired and hungry soldiers. Only four men accompanied Sir Godfrey into the city.

"Most of what the old Rabbi predicted has come to pass," thought Sir Godfrey, "but he was wrong about one thing: I have four men with me, not three."

The thought that he had proved Rashi wrong made the knight feel more optimistic. Sir Godfrey rode his exhausted horse through the city gates with his four knights galloping behind him.

✡ ✡ ✡

Just then, he heard a crashing sound and a loud cry. Turning round, he saw a huge rock hit one of his four knights, who fell to the ground dead.

It was a very quiet Sir Godfrey who dismounted outside the synagogue.

Rabbi Rashi came out to meet him – and the knight hung his head.

"You are a wise man, Rashi. You told me the truth and I was too much of an arrogant fool to listen. Now I am a broken knight."

"You have led many people to their

deaths, Sir Godfrey. Because of you, there are widows and orphans all over Europe. In your quest for military glory you have caused great suffering. Was it worth it – to be king for just three days?"

Sir Godfrey looked at the ground and shook his head.

"Rashi, I see that I have lived a bad, sad life. From now on I will give up fighting, and instead use all my energy and money to help the poor and the suffering."

And so it was that the knight completely changed his way of life. Rabbi Rashi died soon afterwards, but his writings and words of wisdom are still read to this day.

The Coat of Memories

Joseph was a young tailor who worked in his father's shop. Day after day he made clothes of grey, black and brown cloth. Often he thought to himself, "How wonderful it would be to have a coat of many colours like my namesake in the Bible. These dark colours are all very well, but something bright would be a joy to behold."

So Joseph spent as little as possible, saving pennies in a tin.

One day, he went walking in the market and saw a marvellous roll of cloth. It was blue flecked with red and green and orange and yellow. Joseph's eyes lit up. This was the cloth he wanted! So he spent all his savings and bought the cloth and took it back to his father's shop. Every night for a week he sat up late and cut and stitched a coat from the colourful cloth, and when it was finished, he tried it on.

When he looked in the mirror, he liked what he saw.

"What a fine fellow I look in this! It's a magnificent coat. I can't wait to wear it in the street. Everyone will notice me."

So the next day Joseph went out in the street. It was wet and cold but Joseph didn't care. He walked around enjoying all the attention he was getting. Then he saw a young woman without a coat shivering in the rain, and he ran over to her.

"Please let me wrap my coat around you, or you will catch your death of cold."

The girl smiled and took the coat, and Joseph walked her home. Within two years, Joseph and the girl Anna were married.

At his wedding, Joseph addressed the guests:

"For this wonderful bride I have to thank my coat of many colours, through which I met my Anna."

Anna and Joseph were very happy, and had two lovely daughters whom they loved dearly.

Joseph continued to wear his coat until, one day, he noticed bits of it were fraying and other bits were full of holes.

"Anna," said Joseph sadly, "my dear old coat, which made my father proud and brought us together, is worn out. There is nothing left, nothing."

"Nonsense," replied Anna. "There are enough good bits left to make a warm jacket."

"My dear, dear wife, you are absolutely right. I shall give my old coat new life by turning it into a jacket," smiled her husband.

When the jacket was finished, it looked very elegant and Joseph loved to wear it. When it snowed, he would wrap his daughters cosily inside the jacket and take them out to feel the snowflakes falling on them. The jacket lasted for years, until Anna said one day:

"Joseph, I know you don't want to hear this – but that jacket really is worn out."

Joseph looked at the jacket and sighed.

"You are right, my love, but this jacket always makes me think of happy times with our children. Now there is nothing left – nothing."

Then he looked at the jacket again.

"No, that's not quite true. There is just enough left to make a me a warm cap for the winter."

So Joseph cut and stitched until he had a fine hat.

During times of hardship and food shortages, Joseph and his family would go to the woods to look for something to eat. Whenever they found some mushrooms or berries, Joseph would take his cap off and fill it up, and somehow the family managed to survive.

Finally the hat wore out.

"Oh, Anna," wept Joseph. "Look, my old cap, that helped us through the hard times, is gone. There is nothing left, nothing."

"That's not quite true," said his wife, looking at the cap. "If you were to cut the good bits very carefully, you could make a pretty bow-tie."

So that is what Joseph did, and he wore it everywhere – to his daughter's weddings and to the parties of his many grandchildren. The grandchildren always wanted to play with the bow-tie, which they called "Grandpa's butterfly".

One day, when he was very old, Joseph lost the bow-tie and though he searched and searched, he could not find it anywhere. Heartbroken, he took to his bed and refused to eat.

"My bow-tie was the last thing left from that cloth. It is like losing an old friend. Now there is nothing left at all – nothing."

Anna thought for a moment. Then she asked her daughters to bring all their children over to the house.

The children stood round their grandfather's bed.

"Grandpa, Grandpa," they cried. "Tell us the story of your coat of many colours."

"I can't," wept Joseph. "It is too sad."

"Oh please, Grandpa," chorused the children. "Tell us about meeting Grandma and playing in the snow and gathering berries and dancing at all the weddings. Tell us about wearing the butterfly."

Still Joseph lay there and said nothing.

"Grandpa," said the youngest child, "do you think the butterfly flew away and is now flying from flower to flower, and that it feels happy when it remembers us?"

Joseph sat up and laughed, and pulled the child into his arms.

"You are right, my child, the butterfly did fly away – but the memories did not! I have been a foolish old man. The last bit of my lovely coat may have gone but the stories have not. They will live on in our family for ever."

And that is what happened. The story of Joseph and his many-coloured coat was passed on, like all the best things, from generation to generation.

The Prince Who
Thought he was a Rooster

Once long ago, there was a very strange country. What made this place so odd was that all the people there spent their time dressing up in the finest clothes they could find, and walked around showing off to each other. The Prince in this strange land was everything a prince should be – he was very brave and handsome and clever and so it seemed natural that he should be the best dressed and the biggest show-off of all.

But underneath his confident exterior, the Prince had a terrible secret. This secret began to bother him more and more until he stopped showing off and sat in a corner on his own and looked miserable. No matter how hard they tried, no one could cheer up the Prince.

"I'll give a banquet specially for him," the King told the Queen. "We'll all dress up in our very best clothes and eat the most delicious food."

Reluctantly, the Prince came to the banquet,

but sat looking miserable, silently picking at his food.

"You're not eating, my boy," commented the King, "Can I get the royal chef to make you another dish?"

The Prince stood up, "Father, I'm sorry, but I have to tell you and the court the truth. I am not the fine, handsome, clever, brave prince that you think me. No, not at all. I am a rooster. *Cock-a-doodle-doo!*"

Everyone stared at the Prince in amazement, and then they applauded. "The Prince is joking," they laughed. "A rooster indeed! That's a good one!"

But when the Prince took off his clothes and began to walk like a rooster, and to pick up seeds and bugs from the floor and shout *Cock-a-doodle-doo!* everyone was shocked.

"He's off his head!" muttered the courtiers. "Completely nuts! He's lost the plot."

"My son is a lunatic, a royal lunatic," groaned the King in despair.

"Do something, my love," wept the Queen. "I cannot bear to see our son behave like this."

So the King announced: "Anyone who can cure my son will be rewarded beyond his wildest dreams," and he sent his royal heralds through the length and breadth of the land with this proclamation.

Doctors, magicians, witches and faith healers from all over the world came to the court with pills and potions and cures, but no one could do anything about the Prince. The King and Queen were beside themselves with worry,

"Can no one help?" cried the King at dinner one night. "I can't stand it another minute."

"Your Majesty, I think maybe I could cure His Highness the Prince," came a voice.

"Who said that?" demanded the King.

A small man came out of the shadows.

"It's me, Joseph. I work in your kitchens doing the washing up. Your Majesty, I have an idea: leave me alone with the Prince for a week and things will change."

The King wasn't sure, but he was willing to give anything a chance. So the Rooster Prince and Joseph were put in a room on their own.

Joseph took off all his clothes and began to walk around like a rooster. He pecked at the ground, and pretended to shake his feathers, and shouted *Cock-a-doodle-doo!*

For two days the Prince ignored him, but on the third day, when the Prince began his regular crowing, Joseph said, "You have a terrific *cock-a* and a pretty good *doodle*, but you really do need to practise your *doo*."

The Prince looked puzzled.

"But roosters can't talk," he complained.

"Well," replied Joseph, scratching on the ground, "it so happens that I am a rooster who can talk – and why not?"

After that, Joseph and the Prince had many conversations about the things roosters talk about – seeds and feathers and hens and sunrises.

A few days later, Joseph woke up and gave a loud *Cock-a-doodle-doo!* then walked across the room and ate a caterpillar.

"You can't do that," objected the Prince. "Roosters can't walk like people."

"Well, I happen to be a rooster who can walk like a person. And why not?" Joseph told him.

Soon the Prince and Joseph were walking around like everyone else and having regular chats.

The next day, Joseph put his clothes on.

"Why are you doing that?" asked the Prince. "Roosters don't wear clothes."

"Well, I happen to be a rooster who wears clothes," Joseph informed him. "Not much different from feathers really, but more comfortable."

The day after that, Joseph asked for some food to be brought from the royal menu. As he sat eating, the Prince watched.

"Why don't you have some of this?" Joseph said to the Prince. "Seeds and insects are all well and good, but every rooster needs a change now and again."

At the end of the week, the King came down to see Joseph and the Prince. When the door was flung open and the King saw his son dressed and eating food from a plate and chatting away, he wept with joy.

"My son is a prince again!" he shouted, "Declare a national holiday!"

The Prince looked horrified,

"What's my father talking about? I'm a rooster, not a Prince."

"Ah well, you see, when people see you talking and walking like a prince, dressing and eating like a prince, they think you are a prince. The important thing is that you know who you are. Let everyone else think what they like."

But the King glared at Joseph,

"My son still thinks he's a rooster," he shouted. "You said you'd cure him, but the boy still thinks he's a rooster. I'll have you hung up by your ears, you cheat. You said you'd make him better."

"But he is better," cried Joseph. "When he thought he was a prince, he was a show-off. Then he became silent and depressed, and then he went mad. But look at him now – he is happy and relaxed."

"That's true," agreed the King, "but the silly fellow still believes he's a rooster."

"Why don't you look at it like this," suggested Joseph. "When your son thought he was a prince, he showed off like a rooster. He was horrible – 'I'm the cock of the walk,' and so on. Now that he thinks he is a rooster, he is quiet and modest and polite, in fact he acts like a perfect prince. Which do you prefer?"

The King smiled and nodded.

"You're right, Joseph. What a wise man you've turned out to be. For healing my son, when doctors couldn't, I will give you a bag of gold and my undying gratitude. You have served your king, your country and your prince well."

So the Prince went on thinking he was a rooster but behaved like a prince. And when he became king, Joseph remained his main adviser — and so all was well.

The Hundred
Faces of the Tsar

Long long ago, in the vast kingdom of Russia, lived a poor Jewish farmer called Frankel. From dawn until dusk Frankel laboured in the field, and at the end of the day he had just enough to eat. Life didn't change much for Frankel from one year to the next, and he was content to get by scratching a living and just enjoying being alive.

✿ ✿ ✿

One warm day, Frankel was working in the fields, singing merrily to himself and feeling the sun on his face and the song of the birds in the trees, when he heard the sound of a horseman. People rarely rode anywhere near Frankel's tiny patch. Somewhat surprised, he looked up. There, towering over him, splendid in his robes of gold and velvet lined with ermine, was the Tsar, the ruler of all the Russias.

Frankel jumped up, pulled off his hat and bowed low to the Tsar.

"Good day, my fine fellow!" cried the Tsar of all the Russias. "Don't look so surprised. It is a lovely day and your monarch, like every other Russian, rejoices to see the spring. I love to ride out and feel the sun on my face and the wind in my hair and talk to my subjects."

"I am more honoured than I can say, Your Majesty," stammered Frankel.

The Tsar looked long and hard at Frankel and then said, "Tell me, how is it that your hair is white but your beard is black?"

"I've never thought about it, Your Majesty, but maybe it is because I have had my hair since I was a baby. My beard is newer – I have only had it since I was thirteen and became a man."

"Ha!" shouted the Tsar, and burst out laughing, "That question has been bothering me for years, and now a simple Jewish farmer has given me a logical explanation. I thank you."

Frankel bowed low again." I am so happy to have been able to help my Tsar."

"I want you to promise me, on pain of death," demanded the Tsar, "that you will tell no one of this conversation. Do I have your word?"

"You do, Your Majesty. Not until I have seen your face a hundred times will I reveal our conversation to anyone."

"Good, excellent," called the Tsar, and he threw a coin to Frankel and rode off.

Arriving back at his palace, the Tsar summoned all his advisers.

"If any one of you can come up with a good explanation as to why a man's hair may go white but his beard stays dark, that person will be my chief adviser and loaded with riches beyond his wildest dreams."

All the advisers rushed off to libraries to try to answer the question, but no one came up with a good explanation.

Then one man thought to himself, "The day he came up with that question, our Tsar went out for a ride. As I recall, His Majesty rode off to the great forest in the west. I shall go in that direction, too, and see what I can discover."

After riding for a few hours, the adviser saw

Frankel labouring in his field.

"Good day, my good man. I am an adviser to the Tsar. Tell me, have your seen His Royal Highness recently?"

"That I have," replied Frankel.

"And did you tell him why a man's hair may go white while his beard can stay black?"

"That I did," answered Frankel.

"Tell me the answer you gave," demanded the adviser.

"That I cannot do," said Frankel, shaking his head, "for I promised His Majesty not to reveal it to anyone."

"Oh come on, man," said the adviser impatiently. "I need to know this. What can I do to make you change your mind?"

"You could give me one hundred gold coins," Frankel told him, "each one with the Tsar's face on it. Then I will tell you."

The adviser handed over the money. Then, much to the adviser's surprise, Frankel emptied the bag of coins on to the road and looked at each one for a second.

"Hurry up, man," snapped the adviser. "Do you think I am trying to cheat you? Impudent dog! Come on, what exactly did you say to His Majesty?"

Once Frankel had finished, he told the man exactly what he had said to the Tsar. Thrilled, the adviser rode back to the palace at top speed, rushed to the Tsar and revealed what Frankel had said.

Much to the adviser's surprise, the Tsar exploded with rage.

"That wretched Jew Frankel! He promised never to reveal the answer he gave me. Bring the miserable farmer to me immediately and prepare a firing squad. Those who betray the Tsar shall pay with their miserable lives!"

The soldiers rode off to fetch Frankel and he was dragged into the Tsar's throne room in chains.

"You deceitful wretch!" shouted the Tsar, "Before I have you shot, tell me why you betrayed our secret?"

"Your Highness, I swore never to reveal anything until I had seen your face one hundred times. I have here a hundred coins, each with your head on it, and I have looked at every one, so I have indeed seen your face one hundred times. There was no betrayal, Your Majesty."

The Tsar stared at the farmer for a minute, then started to laugh.

"Take the chains off this man," he ordered the guards. "No one is so wise and no one makes me laugh so much. I need men like him around me – witty and fearless. My good friend Frankel, you must move into the palace and be my chief adviser."

So that is what happened. And Frankel became rich and powerful and helped the Tsar to rule wisely.

The Silent Princess

"Can no one get my daughter to speak?" shouted the King. "The girl hasn't uttered a word for years. She shall marry the man who can get her to speak — even if it's just one word."

"Your Highness," said his Vizier, "why not send messengers to every part of your realm offering your daughter in marriage to the man who can break her silence?"

"Do it," ordered the King. "Anything is better than never hearing my daughter's voice. But any man who tries and fails will lose his head."

So messengers went all over the kingdom announcing the King's offer.

Among those who heard the announcement were the three sons of a Jewish widow.

Solomon, the eldest, immediately decided to

take his chance and have a try.

"I shall go to the Princess," he said. "I am sure I can make her speak."

"My son, I beg you, don't take such a crazy risk," pleaded his mother, weeping. "Whatever makes you think the Princess would talk to you?"

"Oh, Mother," laughed Solomon, "I am so handsome that all the girls want to talk to me. Why should a princess be any different? And when I am the King's son, we will all be rich and comfortable."

In spite of his mother's tears, Solomon went to the city and demanded to be allowed to speak to the Princess. He was taken to the Princess's chamber and for hours he chatted and flirted and danced and sang, but the Princess remained totally silent.

The next morning Solomon was beheaded and his head was put on a spike on the city walls.

After that, the messengers again went all over the country with the King's offer.

Abraham, the widow's second son heard the announcement and decided to try his luck.

"My son, my son," pleaded his mother. "You saw what happened to your brother Solomon. You boys are all I have. I implore you – forget that foolish Princess."

"Come on, Mother," said Abraham. "You know that I'm the brains of the family. Solomon was handsome but he was a bit thick. I will make the Princess so interested in what I have to say that she will not be able to resist talking back. You'll see, Mother. And when I am the King's son, we will live in a big house and never have to worry again."

So Abraham went off and, like his brother, was taken into the Princess's chamber, where he talked and talked and told her all manner of interesting things – but could not get her to reply.

Then, like his brother, he was beheaded and his head put on a spike.

When the King's messengers were sent out yet again to the four corners of the realm, the youngest son Saul decided to try as his brothers had done. His poor mother was distraught, and screamed and clung on to her youngest child.

"Mother," said Saul firmly, "I have to go and avenge my brothers, but unlike them, I will return." Then he picked up a candlestick, put it in his pocket, and leaving his grieving mother, he set off to the city.

When Saul arrived, he saw the heads of his brothers on the city walls.

"You are not forgotten, Solomon and Abraham," he called to them.

Saul announced to the King that he wanted a chance to speak to his daughter.

"Are you not put off by the fate of your brothers?" asked the King in amazement.

"No, Majesty – for I am convinced I can get the Princess to talk," answered the boy.

"Your poor mother," commented the King. "But it is your decision."

So Saul was taken into the Princess's chamber.

For an hour Saul said nothing and neither did the Princess. Then he took out a candlestick and started talking to it. The Princess stared at him for a while as he talked animatedly to the candlestick. Then she said: "Are you mad, or what, talking to a candlestick?"

Saul smiled.

"Maybe I am, but my candlestick and I are old friends. Now, candlestick, old chum, you have helped me avenge my two brothers – because the Princess has spoken."

The guards, who had been hiding behind a screen listening, came out and said, "We heard you, Princess. You spoke. Oh, how happy your father will be!"

And Saul and the Princess were taken before the King.

"This is wonderful!" cried the King. "I will keep my part of the bargain. You shall marry my daughter."

"But I don't want her," Saul told the astonished court. "That girl caused the death of my two brothers and no doubt many others. Why would I want to be married to a woman so stupid and cruel?

I shall go back to my mother and tell her that my brothers are avenged and that there will be no more executions – all because of a silly princess."

And Saul walked out of the palace and home to his mother, who wept with delight when she saw him.

"But why no princess?" she asked.

"Because," Saul told her, "I want to marry a sensible girl who loves me and whom I love, not someone who plays stupid games with other people's lives. Mother, I shall marry Hannah from the village and give you many, many grandchildren to make up for the sons you have lost."

And with that, he gave his mother back the candlestick and walked over to Hannah's house to tell her the whole story.

So Hannah and Saul were married and had many children.

As for the Princess, her story was told far and wide, and no man ever asked her to marry him after that!

Sources

The Chilli Champion – *Morocco*
Retold from Moroccan oral versions and from *Jewish Folktales*, selected and retold by Pinhas Sedeh (Anchor Books, 1989).

No Room to Swing a Cat – *Russia*
Retold from a story entitled 'An Overcrowded House' in *My Grandmother's Stories: a collection of Jewish folk tales*, Adèle Geras (Alfred A. Knopf Books for Young Readers, 2003), and also from *A Treasury of Jewish Folklore*, Nathan Ausubel (Crown Publishing, 1989).

The Golem of Prague – *Former Czechoslovakia*
Retold from *The Golem of Old Prague*, Michael Rosen (Scholastic, 1990), based in turn on a story published in *Galerie der Sippurim* (Wolf Pascheles, Prague, 1847).

Friends for Life – *Tunisia*
Retold from a 17th-century story by Rabbi Menachem Lugano, and from *Jewish Folktales*, Pinhas Sadeh Schocken (Israel and Doubleday, New York, 1989). Different versions are told all over the world, including one version in the *Arabian Nights*.

How Does it Feel? – *Poland*
Translated and adapted from *Royte Pomerantsen: a Collection of Jewish Humor*, Immanuel Olsvanger (Schecken Books, New York, 1947).

King for Three Days – *Germany*
Retold from *Jewish Fairy Tales and Legends*, Aunt Naomi (Amercon Ltd, 1991).

The Coat of Memories – *Russia*
Retold from a story entitled 'Just Enough' in *Fifty Two Wisdom Tales from Around the World*, Elisa Pearmain, www.wisdomtales.com.

The Prince Who Thought he was a Rooster — *Poland*
Also known as 'The Turkey Prince', retold from *The Stories of Rabbi Nachman of Bratslav*, www.pinenet.com; and from *The Prince Who Thought He Was a Turkey*, Gedaliah Fleer, www.hasidicstories.com.

The Hundred Faces of the Tsar — *Russia*
Retold from a story entitled 'The Faces of the Czar' in *A Treasury of Jewish Folklore*, Nathan Ausubel (Crown Publishing, 1989).

The Silent Princess — *Morocco*
Retold from Moroccan oral versions. Similar stories can be heard in Iran, Yemen and Tunisia.

ANN JUNGMAN

Ann Jungman was born in London and still lives there.
After qualifying as a barrister she did supply teaching, then
switched to be a primary school teacher, before starting to
write for children. Over a thirty-year period Ann has
published well over a hundred books. Most of the books are
funny stories about monsters lost and confused in a modern
setting – she is probably best known for her marvellous series
Vlad the Drac – but recently she has been writing more
serious books for older children. Ann spends part of
every year in Australia and is the founder
and Director of Barn Owl Books.

MORE FICTION FROM
FRANCES LINCOLN CHILDREN'S BOOKS

Ghaddar the Ghoul
and other Palestinian Stories

Sonia Nimr
Illustrated by Hannah Shaw
Introduced by Ghada Karmi

Why do Snakes eat Frogs?
What makes a Ghoul turn Vegetarian?
How can a Woman make a Bored Prince Smile?
The answers can be found in this delicious anthology of
Palestinian folk stories. Sonia Nimr's upbeat storytelling,
bubbling with wit and humour, will delight readers
discovering for the first time the rich
tradition of Palestinian folklore.

ISBN 978-1-84507-523-1

The Great Tug of War

Beverley Naidoo
Illustrated by Piet Grobler

Mmutla the hare is a mischievous trickster.
When Tswhene the baboon is vowing to throw
you off a cliff, you need all the tricks you can think of!
When Mmutla tricks Tlou the elephant and Kubu
the hippo into having an epic tug-of-war, the whole
savanna is soon laughing at their foolishness.
However small animals should not make fun of
big animals and King Lion sets out to teach
cheeky little Mmutla a lesson…

These tales are the African origins of America's
beloved stories of Brer Rabbit. Their warm
humour is guaranteed to enchant new readers
of all ages.

ISBN 978-1-84507-055-7

Give Me Shelter

Edited by Tony Bradman

Sabine is escaping a civil war…
Danny doesn't want to be soldier…
What has happened to Samir's family?

Here is a collection of stories about children
from all over the world who must leave their
homes and families behind to seek a new life in a
strange land. Many are escaping war or persecution.
If they do not escape, they will not survive.

These stories, some written by asylum seekers
and people who work closely with them, tell the
story of our humanity and the fight for the most
basic of our rights – to live.

ISBN 978-1-84507-522-4

Christophe's Story

Nicki Cornwell
Illustrated by Karin Littlewood

Christophe has a story inside him – and this
story wants to be told. But with a new country,
a new school and a new language to cope with,
Christophe can't find the right words. He wants
to tell the whole school about why he had to leave
Rwanda, why he has a bullet wound on his waist
and what happened to his baby brother, but has
he got the courage to be a storyteller?
Christophe must find a way to break through
all these barriers, so he can share his story
with everyone.

ISBN 978-1-84507-521-7

First Girl

Gloria Whelan

When a second daughter is born to Chu Ju's family,
they decide that the baby must be sent away.
Chinese law dictates that a family may have only two
children, and tradition dictates that one of them must
be a boy. Chu Ju knows that she could never allow
her baby sister to go, so she sets out in the middle
of the night on a remarkable journey
to find a home of her own.

ISBN 978-1-84507-594-1

Butter-Finger

Bob Cattell and John Agard
Illustrated by Pam Smy

Riccardo Small may not be a great cricketer –
he's only played twice before for Calypso Cricket Club –
but he's mad about the game and can tell you the
averages of every West Indies cricketer In history.
His other love Is writing calypsos. Today is Riccardo's
chance to make his mark with Calypso CC against
The Saints. The game goes right down to the wire
with captain Natty and team-mates Bashy and Leo
striving for victory, but then comes the moment
that changes everything for Riccardo…

ISBN 978-1-84507-376-3

Shine On, Butter-Finger

Bob Cattell and John Agard
Illustrated by Pam Smy

Calypso and cricket come together in the
Island's Carnival, and Riccardo has to choose
between his two passions. He has been invited
to sing at the annual Calypso Final, competing
against the most famous singers on the Island,
and amidst the pan bands, the masqueraders and
the stick-fighters he discovers why the singing
competition is called 'Calypso War'. Meanwhile
his team mates at Calypso Cricket Club are playing
the most important game in their history and
their new captain Bashy has a lot to learn
in a very short time...

ISBN 978-1-84507-626-9